The Travel Tapestry

Flairs and Glairs

Publication House

Disclaimer

This is a work of fiction and solely represent the thoughts of the corresponding authors of the articles. Our editors have tried their best to edit the content of all the authors and check the plagiarism.

All the write-ups in this book are unique and are only published in this book.

In case any plagiarism or error is found, only the author is responsible alone, and not the publisher or the Compilers.

Cover Designing and Book Formatting
Shubham Shah

Acknowledgement

Our primary thanks to our God. We are blessed with the energy to be able to complete this anthology.

We are also thankful towards our whole team of "Flairs and Glairs Publication".

Surbhi Gupta

I Offer my heartfelt gratitude to my Parents- Mr. Girish Gupta and Mrs. Neeti Gupta for always motivating and supporting me, in every aspect of my Life. Love to my friends and extended family as well, who keeps showering their Love and Blessings upon me.

Thankyou all the Co-authors , without your support we would never be able to complete this anthology.

Co-Authors

Shubham Shah (Founder Flairs And Glairs)
Ishani Agarwal (Co Founder Flairs And Glairs)
Surbhi Gupta (Compiler)

PART-1

1. Akanksha Sinha
2. Alex Mageto
3. Arjun Dixit
4. Arun Kashyap
5. Baisakhi Das
6. Diksha Motwani
7. Dipti S.
8. Dr. Ratna Priyanka Bhallamudi
9. Haneefah Abdulrahman
10. Hema Kirthiga J
11. Himanshu Ranjan
12. Isha Agrawal
13. Jasmine Panda
14. Jonmoni Dutta
15. Kamna Tank
16. Lavanya Venugopal
17. Madhubala Mahabaleshwar
18. Madhu Singh
19. Neha Singhania
20. Oke Damilola
21. Prachi Gupta
22. Pragyan Panda
23. Pratham Mittal
24. Prittam Bhattacharyya

25. Shijin Ravi C
26. S. Sree Navya
27. Sujitha Ramalingam
28. Sweta Kanodia
29. Tanmayee Pani
30. Vrinnda Gupta
31. Zainab Raees

PART- 2

32. Abhilash Sharma
33. Amanjot kaur
34. Amruta Thakare
35. Hina Patel
36. Kuber Sharma
37. Neeti Gupta
38. Padma Srivastava
39. Priyanka Khunt
40. Sahina Ghugha
41. Sarabjot Purba
42. Sarvesh Upadhyay
43. Shadab Jahan
44. Sheikh Mohammad Junaid
45. Shipra S Gupta
46. Shivika Sharma
47. Shresth Bhargava
48. Shruti Mahajan
49. Tanishka Srivastava
50. Vipul Sune

Shubham Shah

(Founder- Flairs and Glairs)

Shubham Shah, entrepreneur at "Flairs & Glairs" a brand with dynamics in events organizing and cultural educational pan INDIA, He is a 26yr. old guy who recently has entered, the digital platform of imprinting emotions. He has initiated with his own open mic platform to help budding poets and aspiring writers under his brand named as "Teekhe Zasbaaat" He is a commerce graduate from Bhagalpur City of Bihar.
He says Writing has impersonated him since childhood and he has now been writing for over a decade!
Cooking, on the other hand, is his passion! He also mentions, trying out new things just tickles him!
When asked sir, Why SPICY EMOTIONS?

He smiled and added, "agar jasbaat teekhe na ho toh wo jasbaat kaha" Spices are all that blends! So do his words!

As a chef, he presents to you his dish! Hot and freshly served! Taste it! Feel it! Enjoy it! You can also find his writing in the Solo book "Teekhe Zasbaaat" and 70+ anthologies. With his passion to explore opportunities across Platforms he is working with keen devotion and We wish him all the very best for his future ventures

Share your reviews on his

INSTAGRAM

@spicy_emotions
@shubham4shah

Or via email on

shubham2shah@gmail.com

To stay tuned to his work and opportunities follow his business Handles

INSTAGRAM   FACEBOOK   YOUTUBE

@flairsandglairs
@teekhezasbaaat

WEBSITE:

https://flairsandglairs.in/
https://flairsandglairs.com/

Ishani Agarwal

(Co Founder- Flairs and Glairs)

Ishani Agarwal
Born and brought up in Kolkata, she has done her schooling and college from here itself. She is doing her post-graduation at the moment. Ishani loves talking to people around, and is excited for this new beginning of hers! Been a Compiler for 35+ Anthologies, and in the process for more, also, co-authored in 100+ Anthologies, Ishani is very Happy with how her life is turning out now!
Insta handle: Ishani_agarwal_quotes

Surbhi Gupta

(Compiler)

Surbhi Gupta, born and raised in Punjab, is currently a Law Student , B.Com honours graduate and an enthusiastic writer as well. She is also working as Project Head for Flairs And Glairs Publications. Having a Lawyer's mind and a writer's heart, her writings are sui generis, relatable, and inspiring. She is part of various writing events , communities and anthologies as both compiler and co-author. Various achievements in academics , Legal events and writing platforms are feathers in her cap. Sight and smell of her own book someday is what she aspires to achieve as a writer.

Instagram Handle- @surbhi_writes
Email Id- surbhigupta855@gmail.com

A Monastery in Manali

Himalayan Nyinmapa Tibetan Buddhist Monastery Manali
A narrow street was taking me to a place, they said to bring peace. As I kept walking, I entered a place, with lush greens, my eyes met a huge, beautiful edifice, can be called an epitome of aesthetics, seemed like a rich tapestry covering the entire structure.

Beautiful historic places have always captured my heart, but this time, there was a divine aura present which was flowing around, blending with sweet breeze.

On entering the holy abode with my bare feet, I found Lord Buddha's statue, magnificently ruling the place. The statue occupied two stories.

An urge to forget all the happenings of world, and close eyes, to understand the real meaning of life, to avail few minutes of calmness that will cleanse a person, resides inside. It feels as if on opening the eyes, Lord Buddha ' s statue, Guru Padma Sambhava's along with others will come to life , to bless you.

Light illuminating feels as if it has touched the highest skies and reflected around the place. There is soothing aroma of scented candles, olive oils and books .

A room constitutes Prayer wheel with bells at the top and a big architecture outside.

There were hymns being sung, that creates a scenario of an ongoing battle, a battle between good and bad.

At time of departure, I earned myself an experience, the beauty of which I tried to explain in words, but my heart knows, the real feeling, was beyond this world, which will be with me forever.

PART- 1

Akanksha Sinha

Akanksha Sinha is student by profession ,writer as passion. Lives in Patna,Bihar. She loves to portrait feelings by her poetry and quotes,she likes travelling and capturing moments. Heart healer by birth. She is co author of 15+ anthology. She loves to feel the nature. She is passionate &ambitious for her work. Currently, she is been a co-author in several anthologies and compiling her first anthology named "Zindagi-Ek-Ehsaas"...
Instagram Handle @merelabzz

My Dream Vacation

It's the day I've been waiting for
For months and weeks and days
Now, finally, it is time
For me to fly away
I've got my suitcase packed and ready
My passport is in my bag
Soon I'll be stepping out of my house
And quickly hail a cab
Once I've reached the airport
I'll soon take a flight
Arrive at the beautiful city
And see each one of the sights
I'll be sitting at the mountain peak
Enjoying myself
Escape from all work
And all the stress

Spend a day at the spa
Take a dip in the pool
Sleep all day
No worries, no work
Taste every ice cream flavor
Have breakfast in bed
Forget every thing I learned
Or what mom ever said
I'll spend hours in the mall
Certainly plenty of time
I'll buy everything I can
Spend every last dime

I'll have the time of my life
I'll have heaps of fun
I'll treasure all the days
Yes, every single one!

Alex Mageto

Alex Mageto is a writer and a poet from Kenya A lover of basically all Irish work. He is a student aged mid twenties. An extrovert embracing all aspects of art.
Alexmagoma0202@gmail.com

Couldn't find myself
For I was lost in nature
A captive to the landscape
The mountain foot where the tent did sit
Scent to the radiant scape
Beauty in the Indian ocean salt
Toured the Tsavo breeze
Camped on shades of caves
I learned and wrote the aura of Eden
Mastered light in those dark gorges
Lived in the still wild home.
Stole the lions throne
Kissed the art bred by God
Waters above shone at night stars
We hiked on tales around the bone fire at nook
So I vow to ever again quest
The craft of a motherland

Arjun Dixit

Arjun Dixit . He is studying in Bcom final year from Agra university and completed his 12th from a commerce background. He is from Aligarh , Uttar Pradesh . He is young, amazing writer , a kind hearted guy and a person who enthusiastically participates in all extracurricular activities. He is like an open diary who carves His emotions well when it comes to writing .He wants his pen to speak his story. He started writing about one years ago. He write for his own pleasure, don't to be recognized or remembered. Besides scribbling he can count himself as good photographer . He follows a strategy of :- You set the bars, I will raise them. Instagram Handle @the_arjun_dixit

<u>My Travelling Dairy</u>

I travelled a lot of states and cities almost covered all mountain ranges of India...
But the best place I ever found and want again and again to enjoy at that place is Rishikesh.
The best adventure and real thrill I found at Rishikesh...
I did every adventure there River Rafting, Paragliding, Bungee jumping, and Mountain climbing too..
Sitting at the side of floating river is one of the best relaxing place I love..
The sound of floating water through the stones is such a pleasing sound making my mind relaxed...
Long tress on the road side and a river at the another side the scene which nature provides it's hard to find as human constantly cutting all the sides.
Watching out Sunrise and sunset from those mountain ranges and in the evening the prayer sound from the temples and Maha Puja at the Ganga side motivate me from inside...and make my soul pure!
I just have a small dream a small wooden house in the top ranges of the mountain with a river aside and lots of tress besides....

Arun Kashyap

Arun Kashyap belongs to New Delhi, is an English literature student and youth leader of NSS Satyawati College(Eve) D.U. Dedicated to Social Work and passionately inking his feelings for last three years. His nature and values based writing began from Quotes and now his poems are part of Anthologies 'Ek Goonj', ' Lessons to remember', and 'Whimsy of Creation' and he is Author of ' The Essence of Feelings.' A LOTS OF GOOD WISHES FOR WONDERFUL JOURNEY AHEAD

Instagram Handle @ arun_kashyap12official

A Trip, Impossible to possible.

"Artificial beauty is temporary but natural is permanent because it loves caring every heart."
Everyone loves travelling and relishing natural landscapes and it becomes more cheerful in company of loving people. For me, it was difficult to believe at that time when I heard- the words from a member of my team - " Bhaiya is baar to hum kahin bahar jakar hi rhenge kyunki hmari NSS ke itihas me aisa kabhi nahi hua." - these words of my loving NSS team, who can do everything with its dedication. It was the final year of my college life, so after the long discussion we planned a camping trip to Rishikesh, Uttarakhand and finally 23 members were agreed to come with us.
Traveling by train in the early days of February, cheery and foggy weather, and a lot of talking, joking with each other can't be forgotten. After reaching the camping site that happiness was amazing, everyone's expressions were enough to understand that this journey will be more wonderful. Staying in camps at river banks, tracking, playing outdoors games, tracking and having delicious food after getting tired, all these things were a major part of this trip. Tracking was more dangerous than interesting because any little mistake was enough to lose a life.
I was worried and scared by seeing that horrible situation when we all members were fearing, many times we were just saved by blessings and alertness of members. After dealing with the situation I realized that really we can do everything with mutual understanding and beliefs. Listening horrible ghost stories infornt of bonfire by our group was also amazing. The next day we all paid heartfelt thanks to the camp's staff for their wonderful services by dedicating a letter.
The next day we enjoyed river rafting, played musical instruments in a restaurant and roamed ghats of The Ganga

river at Haridwar. All these things were amusing that made this journey fantabulous and memorable. I often feel proud to my whole team who organized this dream journey. - Heartfelt thanks to my team NSS.

Baisakhi Das

Baisakhi Das, a young girl from the city of joy, Kolkata which is situated in West Bengal. She always likes to be with people having interest in arts and literature. She has an amazing passion for writing and has written over 50 contents on Pratilipi, an online social media site based on stories, poems, novels, etc. Her stories and poems are read by over 6.5 thousand peoples and she is the co author of 60 anthology also.

Instagram Handle @baisakhi.das.5686

<u>My Dream Destination</u>

I see off in my yacht
Your finger on the watery horizon
The yacht flies towards the ocean
The sandy beach gradually growing distant and then disappearing
We are in a free land
Where only you and I exist
I so yearn for that kind of time
      The boat sways upon the surface of the sea
While clouds meander across blue skies
I sit in the bow, and you sit at the aft
On all the sides are horizons
The sun gleams down upon as both
You in my eyes and I in yours
I so yearn for that kind of time
      The ocean reflects the sky's bright light
We carefully count the milestones of a lifetime
The dreams of youth and the perplexity of reality
Those times of hills and valleys,sweet and sour,gain and loss
And there still is yesterday,today and tomorrow
I describe my past windblown road
You pour out the myriad bumps and hills along your way
We both are lecturers without an end to our words
We both are tirelessly happy listeners
I so yearn for that kind of time
      Our legs kiss beneath the water
On the surface the spacing arcs grow, then disappear
We hum tunes and sing love songs
Watching the white clouds in their confident procession
Watching the seabirds soaring freely
Laughter splintering into gleaming beams
I so yearn for that kind of time
      Red is the western sky

We kiss and embrace each other, intoxicated
The setting sun sends a sliver of evening light
Winds from the sea blow through your long hair
The most beautiful of all are the scenes we create together
I so yearn for that kind of time

Diksha Motwani

Diksha is a moody girl. She use to write. She use to pen her thoughts when she feels happiest, saddest, depressed. Her pen is her best friend. She believes that writing is a best way to express the thoughts and views. She believes that karma is a bitch. So she keeps herself on peace and calm and let karma do his work. She is a commerce student.(11th standard). She lives in Ulhasnagar, Mumbai. Her dad and her best friend are her motivators. She appreciates the patience level of her dad. She believes that instead of doing a war, do express by penning the thoughts. She is having a goal to be a CA. Besides writing, she practice arts, calligraphy and singing. Instagram Handle @ @radha_1229

My True Love -Katra Travel.

When I was just a five year old, My family and I travelled to Jammu- kashmir, specially Katra . I was literally shocked and at same time I was very happy to travel in train for first time. We reached to katra exactly after 48 hours of travelling from Kalyan junction. After we reached, We had a bit break to sleep and to refresh. After sometime, we started to have a walk to reach our vaishu devi temple. We finally reached after having so much enjoyment in a path along with snowfall. We had a prayer and we started to return back to our hotel. We had a break and started our return journey back to home. Really, I still miss those days, Specially that photo shoots and long walks with family were just amazing. Wanna go once again. It feels like that its My own true love.

Dipti. S

Dipti. S is an aspiring author who aims to become a published author soon. She is exploring in all types of writing. She loves listening to music and doodling. She is an avid reader. She has completed her Bachelors degree in English at Lady Doak College and her Masters degree in English at The American College. She currently resides in Madurai

THE SPLENDOUR OF MUNNAR

As we cross the bends of the Munnar hills,
The lush green grass engulfs us in it's own natural splendor.
As the water that ripples pure in Mattupetty dam.
And, as the beautiful flowers of Mattupetty Garden glitters and glows with colours which seem to welcome us travelers !
And, as the chilled wind overwhelmes us.
The greenery of the tea estate making us wonder at it's beauty while our wanderlust is being fulfilled.
But, despite all this our greed of travelling increases more and more to a point where it cannot be fathomed.
Oh! How fantabulous it was, the tour around Munnar!
A lovely mammoth of bright green.
A lovely Munnar !

MESMERISING KODAIKANAL

The fentablous Kodaikanal with all it's greenery.
Turns out to be a beautiful scenery.
That can be nourished and cherished in your heart for a longer time.
The flowers which buds and blossoms it it's own way.
While my wanderlust increases each and every second.
The wonderful buildings.....
And, the beautiful lake which gives a pleasurable sight with It's own rippling water.
Oh and not to forget the wonderful variety of homemade chocolates which are sold there that are absolutely awesome.
And, roads which are smooth enough to walk up and down.
And, the cute little monkeys with parents are adorable including their tine-tiny ones on the sides jumping about here and there.
And, the chilly whether which blows about a wonderful breeze which would tempt you to fly.
To take flight and to soar high into the sky from where you can adore this whole treasure house of greenery!
Oh! It is a mezmarizing Kodaikanal !

Dr. Ratna Priyanka Bhallamudi

Born to (late) Bhallamudi Venkat Dina mani and bhallamudi vasanta lakshmi. She is a dentist and she got married to Daliparthi venkata girish Sharma. Writing is her hobby and her stress buster

Instagram Handle @Pinks.007

Nallamala forest

Enroute to the shrine
Of our beloved Lord Shiva
A drive through the forest of Nallamala
Famous for its thick vegetation
And the tiger reserve
But the view it offers
Can't be compared to any other
Through the highs and lows
Of the Ghat roads
We get a peek through
Of the upcoming view
Filled with green and grey
I bet there is lot more to see than say
It's a journey everyone would want to make
And this one is something I still remember as if it were yesterday

<u>TIDES of RK beach</u>

Of all the places you visit
Never miss out our beach
The sand here is black,
Look for the waves that lash
So hard that they carry away
People who challenge the mighty waves
However dangerous it may be
This part of the beach
Is packed with people
From every part of our country
This is one heck of an attraction
Where everyone would want to be
To enjoy the view, of evening sun
Taking a dip in the mighty sea
I watched it for around 15 years everyday
Yet, the waves still weave a magical web even today

Haneefah Abdulrahman

Haneefah Abdulrahman is a writer and a poet whose writing and love for arts is immortal. She is the author of the collection of short stories 'The Queens of Age Chains' published on Okada Books. Haneefah has also been published on sites like dailyboom.com.ng, igbocurls.com, thearts-musefair.com, http://www.thecolumnist.com.ng, The Nigerian Review to mention but a few. She manages the blog, trendyneefah.blogspot.com.
Instagram Handle @neefahwords

<u>CALABAR</u>

It is of no use to be stuck in just a place when you can feed your eyes with amazing places (civilized or not), fill your ears with diverse dialects and   use your nose to perceive variety of food, let your tongue enjoy foreign tastes and massage your memory with great experiences.

For the first in the entirety of my life, I was able to travel beyond northern Nigeria. When I boarded the bus , I promised myself that I wasn't going to fall asleep. Fortunately, Some passengers were nice enough to tell me histories of of the places we passed by and others were entertaining with their unnecessary quarrels, friendly jokes and breathtaking stories they tell of themselves. I heard that Calabar, Nigeria is the home of nature and culture, I wasn't satisfied but during my trip, Calabar unraveled it uniqueness and I was drowned in it. Drowned in the dialect, the ever beautiful nature of farmlands, almost everywhere was like a garden in Calabar and that was the most amazing part of it.

I met so many amazing people and cultures entirely different from the north.

<u>DROWNED</u>

If I am asked to become a vagrant
I will go on being a rant with a rank about it
I will drown in every place
As I drowned in Calabar

A city of Mbabong a beautiful
Princess
Her Aura as beautiful as the sky

In Calabar
I met a market with native aroma
Of native food
People with dialect as angels

Life so busy with hope
I drowned and I can still feel
Every bit of blessed water from there drip on me

Hema Kirthiga J

She is Hema Kirthiga J, and her pen name is sparkle. She is professionally a psychologist and passionately a writer. She heals others but writing heals her. She is writer, reader, orator and a believer. She is from Chennai. She lives by the principal of inspire and be inspired. She writes her heart and soul and she deeply believes that the depth of her heart and the nib of her pen are soulfully connected. Writing is an art and she is a proud artist. She loves what she does and loves what she writes. You can reach her at
Instagram Handle @the_pen_queen
Email- inker.sparkle@gmail.com Yourquote – JKM

It was time for the most longing trip!!!
I wrapped up my excitement, joy, and emotions,
To set off to...
Valparai !!!
Also know as 7th heaven!!
Oh my god!!!
The beauty at its best!
It welcomed me with the green bed!
For me to sleep life long!
It poured me Clear water!
For me to bath in happiness!!
The smiling Sparking sunshine!
Is surely contagious, I was smiling like an idiot....
The aroma of nature!!!
Stealing my heart!
Ripping my bone!
Settling in the brain!
Captivating my mind!
Oozing into my soul!
The soul was cleansed!
The mood was enhanced!
I travelled there years before!
But still could not forget the beauty!
It trapped me!
The mother nature at its best!!!
Even if i close my eyes now!!!
I can feel the moment of joy!
The moment of my mumma earth hugging me!!!

Himanshu Ranjan

He is a Sophisticated person. He is Man of Action. He believes that happiness lies within and must be shared to maximum. He believes stars looks more beautiful at Shoulders than at Sky. Nation comes first and then his people and at end his own stuffs.

Jai Hind

Instagram Handle @ himanshuranjan.87

<u>The Journey of Happiness</u>

We Started our journey to Bangalore on Mid of August. The trip in bus was amazing. Being unknown to few class mates gave opportunity to know more. We reached chamundi hills at 05.50 am.Everyone was Waiting for the Sunrise from top of the hill. It was really an eye treat moment.After that we all checked in hotels and then we went to see Mysore Palace, ISKON temple and Brindavan garden. The trip became memorable when while returning back to our places the crush of bus Sat next to me and whole bus eyes was on me. It was really surprising and at the same time good moment to know more about her. Finally I captured tons of memory.

Isha Agrawal

She is Isha Agrawal. She is from the state where garba is in heart and jalebi fafda is life, Gujarat. She is 18 years and currently doing her management studies. Her aim to complete her management studies with masters and to do start up. She wants to become an entrepreneur. Her hobbies are - reading, writing, travelling. She is a writer and she only writes for herself but currently writing in books and publishing her write ups. Instagram Handle @_isha.1110_

Jaisalmer - The Golden City..

The golden day was flowing
And the desert safari was mind blowing..
The golden sunset in golden sand
Looks like god painted a dream land...

Sonar Quila was stunningly carved
And Sam Sand Dunes made me supercharged..
The ride of camel was peerless
And the golden fort made me speechless..

The Gadi Sagar Lake was so beautiful and calm
And the weather so lovely that cannot harm...
The Khuri Sand Dunes filled me with so many memories
And the food made me eat too much without thinking of
calories...
The golden lights of whole city was incredible
The journey and the roads were commendable...
Living in the tents were ineffaceble moments
Smiles, happiness and craziness were main components...
Sunrise from Patwa ki Haveli had a great shine
The golden city has golden memories of mine...

Jasmine Panda

Jasmine Panda is presently pursuing M.Sc. Chemistry from Berhampur University, Bhanjanagar, Odisha, India. She is a Gold Medalist and University Topper in her B.Sc. She is also continuing an internship CSIR-SRTP in IICT Hyderabad. She is a Governor Awardee for Youth Red Cross. She has received All-Rounder Award in her 12th standard. She has been Literary and Cultural Champion in her college days. She has also cracked a campus in Vedanta. She has been appreciated as an anchor in many International events. She has completed Masters in Fine Arts (MFA) from Bangeeya Sangeet Parishad and done a computer course PGDCA. She is an amiable person interested in both Science and Literature. Publishing her own book someday is something which she aspires!

Never Ending Footsteps

My enthralling trip to South India!!!
Magical day and night view of Mysore Palace,
The architectural interior of Bangalore Palace!
Magical was Wonderla and Vrindavan Garden,
An evening in Ooty was no less than heaven!
Ooty's Botanical Garden, the Nature's treasure,
Visiting with family and relatives, a pleasure!
Never ending footsteps....

My memorable trip to North India!!!
Starting our day from Mathura Vrindavan,
With a Divine experience at Akshardham!
Visiting Fatehpur Sikri and the Taj Mahal,
City Palace, Jantar Mantar, Hawa Mahal!
Visiting Red Fort, Lotus Temple and Rajghat,
An exciting tour to the famous India Gate!
Never ending footsteps....
Never ending footsteps....

<u>Pause The Moment</u>

It was on 3rd October, 2019, that my memorable travel trip started from smart city Bhubaneswar to Delhi. Enjoying the cloudy sky and landscape from above, we were welcomed by rain at about 8 pm in the evening. The lodging and accommodation was awesome. The 6-day long trip started from Mathura Vrindavan. The next day, we arrived in Agra, to fulfill my long awaited dream to come face to face with the great architectural wonder, the Taj Mahal. The white glazing marble beauty, with reflecting waters and the green courtyard, against the backdrop of the sky was captivating. Completely immersed in my thoughts, I took rounds of the monument again and again. The first wonder of the world is every bit true to its fame. Such is the enigma of the Taj!

Next morning, after visiting Fatehpur Sikri, we started for Jaipur, visiting Jal Mahal, City Palace, Jantar Mantar, Hawa Mahal, Amer Fort, etc. A day in Akshardham left us with a divine experience! Some of the memorable destinations of the last day were Birla Temple, Rajghat, Red Fort, India Gate and Lotus Temple. It was like "never ending footsteps". Each day of that trip brought new sights and new adventures. Finally after shopping, we returned from Delhi to Bhubaneswar, again welcomed by rain!! So, traveling with family and relatives, I was desparate to "pause the moment" then and there...but in reality, I have paused it in my heart's diary, every bit of an exciting, enthralling and memorable family trip!!!

Jonmoni Dutta

Jonmoni Dutta, is from Dhubri district, Assam. She is pursuing BSc with honors in physics. Apart from this, she likes to express her inner thoughts and feelings through her self composed poems , short stories and quotes in different languages like Assamese, English and Hindi . She is a science student with poetic mind. She is not a established writer but her writings are published in various magazines ,in various anthologies and once in newspaper also.She also likes to read various books and listen music in her free time. Her aim is to become a Professor and a published writer in future. Instagram Handle @d. jonmoni

The Tour - An Unforgettable journey of My Life

In life we all had various memorable things that always remind in our heart . One of such memorable thing of my life was the "Delhi - Rajasthan Tour" from 02-10-2019 to 08-10-2019 under the "Ek Bharat Sreshta Bharat " scheme. The tour was organized by our college. 14 students from each of 14 departments were selected for the tour. And I was only one from our department who was selected for the tour. From then to till now this was the best travel experience in my life. It was my pleasure to be a part of the tour. For the first time, I went out of the house alone for a long trip. The tour was totally conducted by train. It was really a lifetime experience of mine. I learned a lot of things in this journey and visited many historical places of Delhi and Rajasthan. In delhi, we visited Sri - Laxmi Narayan Temple, Rastrapati Bhavan, Parliament House , India Gate, Qutub Minar, Samadhi of Mahatma Gandhi at Rajghat, Lotus Temple, Red Fort etc. And in each spot the tour guide described all the historical and various all other information regarding all the marvelous structures and significance of each and every thing . In Rajasthan, we visited Birla Temple at Jaipur, Pink City in Jaipur, Jantar Mantar, City Palace, Rajasthan Textile Development Co - orporation, Amer Fort, Hawa Mahal, Nagra Shoe Factory, Jal Mahal , Pushkar, Brahma Temple at Pushkar, Ajmer Dorgah etc. The tour guide while visiting in Birla Temple described the rule and culture of it , while visiting the Jantar Mantar the guide described to us how people in ancient days used to calculate data, time just by looking at shadows falling on the instruments and location of stars and also described how those people used to determine the astrological sign of new born babies, while visiting City Palace the guide described about the history of city palace and the various dresses worn by Royal family members on various occasion and also described about the guns and weapons used in ancient days, while visiting Amer Fort the guide described about the history of the fort and various significance of the fort, while visiting the Pink City the guide described how people used to numbered the shops instead of having names there etc. In this way the tour guide beautifully and smoothly decribed all the cultures ,tradition and importance of various marvelous structures while we were visiting those and we all learned much things about Rajasthan that we didn't know before. And I was totally attracted by the beauty of Rajasthan. I also clicked a lot of pictures there for keeping the memories saved. Really it was an unforgettable journey of my life with new experiences of my life.

Kamna Tank

Kamna Tank is a Dietician By Profession and Writer by passion. She loves to Portreys Emotions on paper to encourage ownself about feelings Apart from writing Drawing, Travelling, Listening Music Is her passion She always love to create something new. She Always Ready To Tackle With New World
Instagram Handle @kittykitts2

Journey to Hyderabad

It was the memorable journey of my life because it was unplanned, That day i understand some unplanned trips are best.

Journey start with bulletin board of my college where written about the national seminar going to held in Hyderabad, Firstly i just ignored it because I am not interested in attending seminars.

After few days I got a call from my best friend that she is going to Hyderabad to attend seminar, She asked me too to come but without thinking I just say no to her. She said I know why are you refusing to come with me but who said we are only going Hyderabad to attend seminars, After that we were exploring Hyderabad, there are many place to visit there. After that my whole night spent as sleepless whether I go or not.

Next day morning I discussed with my father and told about this seminar trip, And for the first time i get a chance for long trip, I was super happy that day.

Me and my friend has enjoyed a lot there parks, fort, film city every place are just amazing to roam , The rituals over there was amazing, Every place has its own aroma to attract. From that place I learned so many things. People over there are also very sweet and calm always ready to help.

It was my best journey experience and memorable forever

Lavanya Venugopal

A freelance writer in her own world. Writing is not just about mere talent ,but a form of an emotion...A bibliophile too .Books are patient enough to listen to you when human ears turn deaf...Ever felt alone? Melancholic??If so please take the company of a book .. Wait a novel ..Apart from all this an complete extrovert...Red letter days are those when people walk into your life in a Serendipitous way. They thrill you like a fine poem..Daughter of India !! Lover of the Devangiri language..

Rabindranath Tagore,Emily Dickinson, Helen keller,Anne Frank,Paulo Coelho, Rober Shuller,Arthur Basham,Devdutt Pattnaik..Are all her favourites.. Instagram Handle @thepowerofwriting

Mount Abu- The Glacier In Which I Live

Travelling is a joy which cannot be put by mere words! So am I a travel geek who finds pleasures in the outside world. Every place I visit becomes a part of my heart for the panorama, or the culture that it holds.
So is "MOUNT ABU" the one and only hill station in Rajasthan.

When I visited Mount Abu I was awestruck by it's beauty. From the tranquil gravity to the lovable people everything was worth a million moments!!
"Padharo Mare Desh" the line that drizzles the feel of Patriotism in me!!The beauty present in india is unparalleled!The peaceful Brahma Kumaris reminds that the world still relies on peice and that humanity can never die .The Dilwara Temples are the classic beauties of india!!So is the Somnath Temple which couldn't get destroyed by the "Sultans and Mughals ".
The food though completely vegetarian is extremely scrumptious and worth relishing .So are the busy streets that sell Indian handicrafts and jewelries.
Apart from the tourist spots like lakes, and restaurants it's these places that shows the beauty of Indian Culture that is still alive amidst tha foreign influence!
Never leave a stone unturned by not visiting this Heaven!!

Madhubala Mahabaleshwar

Madhubala Mahabaleshwar in a nutshell - an engineer by education, a technical writer by profession, and a creative writer by passion. Music, books, nature, and meditation nourish her soul.

How can someone not fall in love with you, Hampi?

The land of
A grand and overwhelming history
The remains of wars of egos and strength
The once majestic marketplaces
The crumbling walls
Those empty temples
Some unheard whispers
The soft chirps of the colorful birds
The magnificence of sunsets and sunrises
The mundane day-to-day battles for survival
The paradise of the wandering souls
The serene river
The undefeated rocks
How can someone not fall in love with you, Hampi?

Madhu Singh

Her name is Madhu Singh .she love to write motivational, inspirational, and emotional quotes .She started writing in March 2020 and very soon she became a part of flairs and glairs as a co-author in the face of flairs and glairs she get a bit success in lit age . She is hard-working and determined girl who never give up in any situation and she also make others motivate .she is a simple girl who love to talk and help and care about others . Most of the people called her an innocent girl. She love to enjoy and captured each and every moment of her life .

Instagram handle @Madhusingh4236

My Summer Vacation

My summer vacation was going on very well, Because I came at fatehpur sikri village.

I am back home after having a wonderful time in my village .I found in my village life is clour to nature it was and miracle for me to see all that. In morning we were use to get up early in the morning at 5 o'clock by hearing the voice of peacocks which was like an alarm.

Then I came outside of my house and I saw village people already wake and went to their farm to saw their crops or their animals and then they took out the milk of goat and buffaloes and after 1 week i came back to my home and sharing my wonderful journey with my friends.

Neha Singhania

Hello, introducing Neha Singhania. She is Pursuing CS and a good dancer. Writing is her passion, and she want to be a good known writter .she always try to write on undefined feelings..

Instagram Handle @Dil-e-ehsasss , @neha_singhania_

A trip to Mansarovar.

From the day I got to know about mansarovar.I always want to go there and feel the beauty of nature which all will be in the journey of mansarovar.

I want to travel alone and meet new devotees of shiva and to have conversation with them, being with them and enjoy my ownself.I have a special interest with the people who having a journey of spirituality and on this journey I would love to be with them and want to know about their experiences and spirituality.

As I always heard that the cold and calm atmosphere of mansarover is so attractive and dazzling.

 I want to feel each and every moments of this journey with the core of my heart and sit silently to spent time with my all time buddy i.e.Nature, And meditate there and learn lots of things in this journey.

Special part -to visit the place where shiva resides and go high with that vibes and to touch the place, feel the aura keep everything in my eyes forever and mesmerizing with the sound of beauty.

Sure I will be delightful in this place.

Waiting for that day.

Living this day in my dreams so many times now I want to live in real life.

Oke Damilola

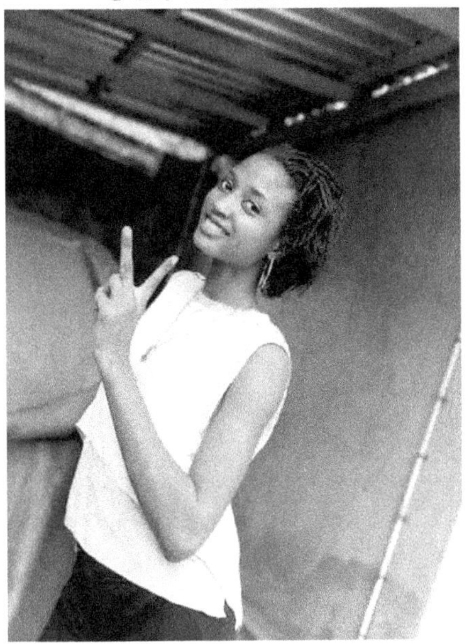

Oke Damilola is a 19 year old Nigerian writer.She started writing as a hobby in the year 2016 and she is very excited to have some of her work published in this book.
Instagram Handle @okedamilola

ZAMBIA

Love brought me to a place surrounded by blacks like me but not blacks like me.

My ears hear tongues so oddly, making no nice tones. In an environment so different from the one I have lived and grown. surrounded with trees and vegetations, with few houses or should I call them huts. There I got to eat a food called nshima and relish. There I got to learn a new culture out of my imaginations . The people around so nice, attitude so kind. But there never like the home I once known.

Love brought me there.

OSOGBO

A travel back to the land of Osogbo, the heart of Osun State, situated somewhere in Nigeria. There I got to visit the city square which left a big scene in my mind, one that shows the picture of human's struggling. The sight of the hustling and bustling of mini blue buses and two legged motorcycles stained the street. Pedestrians and beggars lines and walk the road side to a destination known to them.The skies in the city are ever so clear ever so bright making my eyes go blurry from its radiance. Osogbo, A city I once lived and grown. If you were ever given an opportunity to tour, come visit Osogbo, the city of my heart.

Prachi Gupta

Prachi Gupta is a student of BBA hailing from Allahabad, UP. She is fond of travelling, cooking and watching movies. Beside this, she is a Digital Marketer, writer and a compiler. As, she believes that scribbling on a blank paper can burst out all the hate and makes a person happy. Along with this, she has been a co-author of many anthologies.

Instagram Handle @prachi_gupta_210 or @prachigupta3435

KASMIRI TRIP

I got goosebumps from remembering those days of fun.
Travelling from Allahabad to kashmir and finalizing the slots
or plans.
I couldn't feel the snow, wind and purity here,
Which I felt in those places.
Mountains, hills and valleys,
All were snowy and cold.
Restaurants, resorts and hotels,
All were booked and enrolled.
Those riding, climbing, shooting and skating is still
partialness.
I want to do trekking again,
To rejuvenate myself by hiking, journeying and tramping.

Pragyan Panda

Pragyan is persuing her B.Tech in "Chemical Engineering" from IGIT, Sarang. She's a short girl from Rourkela, Odisha. With fascination of nature, she's a spiritual person who motivates people. She does weird stuff like interacting with non living ones and pens down her mind.
Instagram Handle @quote_love_97.

BADRINATH-THE THRILL

I remembered my day surviving the chills.
Everything was frozen including our meals.
The tap water was icy before it could freeze.
Perhaps I required some thick shield to move with ease.

The steep roads to Badrinath were fierce.
The buses carrying passengers drove really harsh.
Hardly I stopped praying during the journey,
Same was with everyone in the company.

As the altitude increases, I felt suffocated:
The thrill of the peaks felt more elevated.
I could not scream or shout of help;
But was only peering into map.

A crowd of old pilgrims kept on chanting_
"Why am I risking myself?" was my constant asking,
There were regular snow falls and landslides,
The lodges filled with people and their guides.

The ice cap top march ends in two days:
Finally, we reached the top noticing the sun rays:
And then a realisation stuck to me..
"Can I return back safely?"

Pratham Mittal

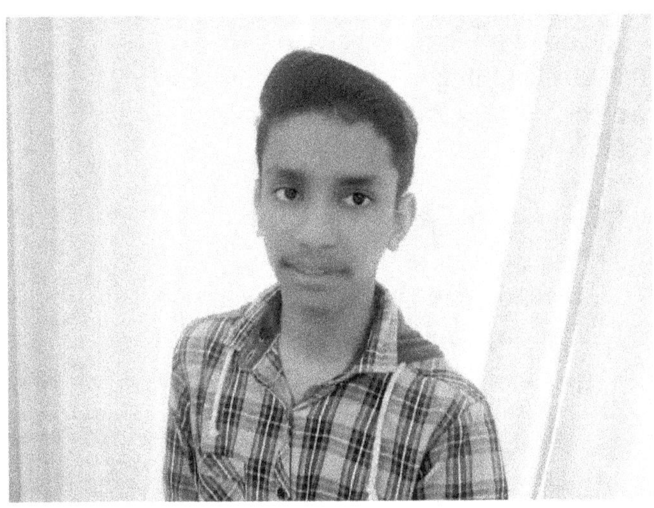

He is very Positive, kind, helpful, friendly and happy soul. His passion is painting and writing. He has won many competitions, published in many books, participated in international writing competitions.
Instagram Handle @_pratham2426

Dream Vacation

You've heard of a "Dream" vacation,
well that is what I'm gonna do.
My Brother and that I on a cruise liner,
which to us is new thing.

This will be the primary straight year
that we've gone on a seven day cruise.
Of all the vacation options I even have ,
it's the one I always choose.

The name of the ship is Carnival "Dream",
the largest in their fleet.
So it's my "Dream" vacation in additional ways than one,
which I feel is pretty neat.

The first stop are going to be in Nassau,
a Bahama paradise.
Next are going to be St. Thomas
I've already been there twice.

The next stop is St. Maarten.
It'll be my third time there.
Even though I have been before,
it's so lovely, I do not care.

At these three stops, I'll just relax,
don't really do this much.
I may go ashore and appearance around,
shop a touch and see the sights and such.

For the various attractions the ship offers,
I just can't say enough.
Excellent shows and things to try to ,

to top them would be tough .

This is my "Dream" vacation,
I always anticipate too.
It's the most relaxed I ever get,
there's nothing I'd rather do.

Prittam Bhattacharyya

Prittam Bhattacharyya is from Kolkata, the city of joy. Currently pursuing a Bachelor's of Computer Applications. Writing is his passion, his way of expressing his innermost emotions. Every now and then he writes stories, poems, and lyrics of songs. He always likes to be a part of any artistic community. To him, art is something which brings people together. He wishes to write many stories and poems in the coming days. He has interest in stuff related to computers and electronics, such as programming, game and graphics designing, and robotics. He has also been a part of over 50 anthologies.

Instagram Handle @Prittam3000.

<u>The Amazing Places Of India</u>

In the bowl of flowers, lies the paradise for trekkers
Mesmerizing sunrises behind the mountains of Ladakh
Feels like god has created his own beautiful art
The undiscovered realm of nature calms our heart

The cascading water that changes its colours
As the sun falls on the water creating its own palette
Cherrapunji gives us one of its beautiful waterfalls
We went out to fill our diaries, exploring the natures as it calls

The towering marvel of nature, a heaven for travelers
Uttarakhand amazes us with its late night's stars
We climbed the grand canyons and campfires at night
We swayed to the Ukulele music as it broke the quite

Long fabled among the travelers for its marvelous beaches
Andaman and Nicobar gives us it flaming purple sunsets
The undisturbed honeymooners' getaway in the middle of the ocean
It's lovely opaque emerald waters fills us with loving emotion

The sea of flora that gives us its refreshing aromas
The valley of flowers is the fairyland with pink flowers
Uttaranchal gives us blue blurry mountains covered with fog
In the garden, we take one of our happiest morning walks

The hill town of God's own country, a haven of peace
Kerala has its sprawling tea plants and artistic towns
The forest looking over the wavy rivers, and birds singing away
Travelling calms our soul and beautifies our coming days

Shijin Ravi C

He is Shijin Ravi C from Kerala. He is pursuing BSc Hons Agriculture graduate. He is a young poet and co-author of many anthologies today. Some of his anthologies are 'The golden words', 'The uncertain periods', 'My success ladder', 'Safar', 'Her voice', 'Positive vibes' etc
Email ID : shijinravi23@gmail.com
Instagram Handle @stolen.pearl

Peaceful Mind

My mind run through the busy world,
Where one never cared others feelings,
Squeezing me like a sponge to dry,
Made me lose my peace beneath my head .

I realized I need a break from then,
Moved all the way to a place of heaven,
The land of beaches and trades apart,
Where you often see foreigners bath .

Through the scents of Goa I walked,
Took me to a place full of heart,
My lips sensed a freedom to laugh,
That I almost forgot where I was .

Like a magic all over the places,
Hailed me to dance in the flow of song,
With the famous drink known there,
I just threw all the pain somewhere.

Down I reached the casino's on fire,
Betting and winning made the night admire,
Seeing all that made me to put a hand,
That I played my share almost to my desire.

Night kept the hunt to run the show,
Reaching my hotel I slept so soon,
Next day after all that fun I woke up,
With a new mind and boosted heart .

S.Sree Navya

Hi this is Navya here. She is A Masters student who is pursuing her Master of Arts degree in Human Resource Management. She loves writing poems and quotes and book reviews.

Instagram Handle @thoughtsofnavs_

My journey to London

My journey to london which is my dream destination was a dream come true! I was so overjoyed to see my dream come true. I visited the clock tower, which is one of the famous destinations in london. The weather was so warm that I felt like being at home. I stayed at Novotel london for the first two days after which we shifted to my cousin's house. We visited Warner brothers studios where Harry Potter was filmed. My sister and I are huge Harry Potter fans so we truly enjoyed going there. We had a blast there.

My journey to Bhutan

Bhutan is a place which everyone should visit. The city of bhutan is so amazing that one would love going there! I loved visiting it. Thimpu is a very nice place in bhutan, the cuisine the Bhutan people eat is so different from what we have. I loved the monasteries and their architecture is something that captivates me and captures my attention. If you haven't visited bhutan please do it's a beautiful place. The people there are so friendly!

My journey to Hyderabad

Every year during Summer holidays or whenever I have holidays I used to visit Hyderabad which is my native place. It's a great feeling when I meet my cousins after a long time. I have fond memories in Hyderabad. It's like my second home. I wish I visit Hyderabad soon because I miss being with my cousins and friends. The feeling of going back to a place you have spent most of your fond memories is nothing but surreal.

Sujitha Ramalingam

This is sujitha.
She is a housewife, at the time of lockdown she found herself with the help of paper and pen.
Instagram handle @stories_of_facts.

My Healness

It's the beautiful island named as ANDAMAN. It occupied with people from different countries and different languages. It has many more islands. Every island has its own speciality like Coral reef, marine algae... It's a great feast to all the beach lovers.

At first, we went to the Cellular Jail, this is the most famous jail. The architecture itself shows how our freedom fighters suffered. Then we visited an island and it's filled with an abandoned old British building.

Then, we went to a beautiful place called Havelock. With all the safety measures, entered into the water activity called scuba diving and we can see all the beautiful creatures under the sea by diving.

It's the last and most memorable day. The most special thing in Andaman is Baratang. Andaman is mostly filled with the forest and sea. In the forest, there are Tribal people. Actually, they are the real Andamanese called as Jaravans... It's just a travelling time from portblair to Baratang. While travelling, by luck you can see some Tribes. And we entered into limestone cave filled with adventure.

Finally, with half-hearted and much more memories, we moved to home town. In this trip, I learned that this world is very big, filled with Wonders and happiness. Travelling is the best one to heal our self.

Andaman – The place where nature still exists and helps to experience many more adventure.

Sweta Kanodia

A company secretary by profession
Writer by thoughts
Instagram Handle @Iamswetakanodia

"A LIFETIME EXPERIENCE TO THE NORTHERN LANDS (UTTARAKHAND)"

Uttarakhand, a state that attracts people of all age group because of its extraordinary holy pilgrimage cities to the most adventurous sporting feels . It looks as beautiful as the morning sunrise, and as vibrant as the setting sun.

I remember riding on the horse's back to view the Himalayan peak that was all soaked up in ice blankets; there were also silver linings in the cloud as if they were talking of their holy abode out and loud.

Those mountains were a treat to eyes and those roads were a roller-coaster ride.

Sitting on the balcony of my hotel room, keeping my leg on the table top, sipping on my hot bowl of noodles, and having the best hot chocolate cupcake at the middle of the night was the only thing seeming right.

I used to stare at those fairy lights that the city used to look at the night.

That spark of getting up and roaming in the most chilly and frosty weather, the happiness of cuddling up in the blanket, the shopping spree that made me feel free, The winds and the breeze, the sky and the stars, the place and its warmth was all so exciting that it felt every bit enticing.

I tried so many sports that happened to be a part of my bucket list when it was all so mist.

It has so many colours and shades but nothing it has that will ever fade.

Of all my travel experiences so far, this one remains pinned to my heart.

Tanmayee Pani

She is a undergraduate student from Gangadhar Meher University, Sambalpur, Odisha pursuing a career in Integrated B.ed. She is a dynamic writer who have been a co author in 10+ anthologies and a published author. She loves to speak her heart out through her mighty words in the form of poems, short stories, shayaris and one liners.
Instagram Handle @t_p9849

My tour to Paradise

It was not long ago me standing amid the beautiful meadows. When I was in between the Himalayan ranges, I was rather confused that they are staring their new visitor, Or it was me who was gazing their beauty and taking in all I could. Those beautiful hillocks and the green valleys they just stole away the heart of a 12 year old such that.. since then I have been dreaming of returning to the same heavenly trip.

All this beauty was of Char Dham Yatra in Uttarakhand. Starting from the chilled Gangotri till the thermal reservoirs of Kedarnath and Badrinath, all were an inseparable part of the trip.

My trip started from Haridwar. We were riding by road to Gangotri glaciers then to kedarnath and Badrinath temple respectively. Just thinking of it brought chills over my body.. because 2 jackets were also not enough to keep me warm. And added to that the long endless queues. I was a child then, had no idea about all these pilgrimage centres, and in all of that I was just staring mother nature. I was always naturalist and found peace with greens. This was a rather golden chance for me.

The best part of my whole trip was when I was on my way to Kedarnath. It's a 14 km trek route from Gauri kund, which we covered using mules. It was a exciting ride when I was scared more than my younger sister who pursuaded me that nothing will happen. Then moving ahead the icy rainfall.. froze us to a greater extent, all were lost whole the journey, Everything was like where is everyone and we are freezing please save us. But all these pain faded away at once when we were in front of the beautiful shrine. Then the way back .. we had a short walk back to Gauri kund and that was the most difficult part of the journey. It was where we were most thrilled ,excited and scared.

All the best memories comes when we are willing to pursue it.. so was this. But must say that this was and will remain the most reminiscing trip of my life forever.

Vrinnda Gupta

She creates visual concepts either by Ink on Parchments or with her typewriter complemented by a late night coffee. She wants to travel places, meet vivid souls and get inspired by the act of Happiness.

Instagram Handle @vrinny_da_pooh

Love Summer Skies and Winter Night:
A Wanderer's First

Life is sporadic, nomadic and a chase of contrast.

We live on highs to ride out our lows, but amidst this push and pull of survival, are we really happy?

Back when I was crooked-tooth, pixie haired and Nancy Drew reading, shy girl, I visited a place close to Utopia. Or at least that's how it seemed to the 10 year old me.

Long willowy trees, mapped our road of ascent to Chamba, a beautiful small alcove of habitat, nestled in the valleys of Shivaliks.

Throughout our drive, much to my mother's dismay, I remember sticking my hand out to touch the marshmallow clouds which seemed so within my reach.

And just as dreamy as those clouds, did the rest of the journey span out to be!

Our rented small cottage sat just on the top of the valley, overlooking vast hills and two crystal clear rivers. Yet, more than the homey cottage, it was the magnificent blue sky that blanketed my fingertips, as I ran down the streets, with fingertips extending above.

My days were filled with stumbling alongside trekkers, down the deep woods as the sun played the most wicked game of hide and seek. And my nights crested with clearest moonlight and contrasting bonfire under which I heated up my nimble fingers (just short of getting burnt), much to my adult camarades amusement.

Looking back upon it, I went there with my curious-wide eyes, shy self and came back with an elated heart.

The same heart that went back to the valleys of Chamba, a decade later, with tired-eyes and mature self. Yet the familiar blue blanket that I once touched with my small fingers, felt just as reachable and pure now, as a Wanderer's First Love.

Zainab Raees

Dear Readers,
If a story is in you it has to come out.
Zainab Raees is a passionate English Honours student. She is a 'Ink Slinger' who contends a constant struggle with her 'Self' within the silent chambers of his spirited psyche. Her words are fueled with underived intrinsic emotions that explain the psychological perspective of simple everyday occurences and events. You can read more of her works
Instagram Handle @good_wishes_to_your_tomorrows
E-mail: zainabraees00@gmail.com

<u>Journey</u>

While in the middle of the magical days of cotton clouds in the silver sky,
And the mornings when grass looked more green and air with sweet scent of wild flowers and plants playfully hitting the nose at intervals
I didn't knew that I was living the dream, cradling on the wings of my aimless spirit throughout this journey silently.
While standing on the valley edge facing the mountains in between my little breaks to the moving, slow life
I didn't knew that I was living the dream that once remained only in the last pages of my notebooks in childhood.
While running through the green wet meadows, sitting around a warm bonfire, shivering and dancing in the full moon nights
I didn't knew that I was living the dream that I once read only in pages of fairy story books from school library.
While breathing one of the pure happiness, watching endless shooting stars from the mountain top, experiencing milky white snow fall
I didn't knew that I was living so much dreams that once gave me sleepless nights in between my bedroom walls.
While climbing the poetic mountains, happily witnessing the sunrise cracks, screaming after reaching at the peak
I didn't knew that I was living this fucking so called 'dreams' that once I wrote in my personal diaries.
And I'm wondering how I grew up
Living big dreams in normal daily basis
Finding joy in everything wild and free
Not realizing when I became one of them in the process!
And now sitting in my home couch
Scrolling my gallery carrying such a colorful memories & wild experiences

I realized that I've became one among the crazy tiny dreams of others, of fellow wanderers
Because now I'm dreaming the 'old monkey me' laughing loud in the mountains holding fresh wild fruits
While I just sit with a cup of black tea in the veranda of my home now!
I see you
You're precious,
You're beyond the dreams,
Loving myself beyond words.
Good Evenings to your memories.
Good wishes to your tomorrow's.

PART – 2

Abhilash Sharma

Abhilash Sharma a 23 year old passionate writer. He belongs to Sonipat , Haryana . He had completed his B.com (voc) recently. He is a enthusiastic person and a sports lover as well .Worked as a co author in about 40+ anthologies inspired by Ishika Arora and Ishani Aggarwal in the field of writing .
 Instagram Handle at @_ankahe_alfaaz_

वो यादों का सफर

वो हसीन पहाड़ों की वादियाँ ,
भुलाती जो ज़िन्दगी की खुमारिया ,

वो मंद मंद सी होती बरसात ,
जो कह जाती अनेको बात ,

वो कानों में बजते गाने ,
याद दिलाते नायाब फ़साने ,

वो ढ़ाबे की कुल्हड़ वाली चाय ,
बना जाती एक अलग सी राय ,

वो सुनहरी सी घुमती सड़कें ,
जो चलती रहती बिना लड़के ,

बस अब हुआ पहुँचने का वक़्त ,
यहाँ के नियम जो है सख़्त ,

कहते है इससे ऋषिकेश ,
मिलते है रब के अनेको वेश ।।

Amanjot kaur

Amanjot kaur. She is Amanjot Kaur with pen name: Khwaab. She is from Punjab. Basically She is a Teacher. She loves to write stories and poetries. She hopes readers will like her content
Instagram Handle @ amanjot_kaur126

कभी आपने एक ख़्वाब देखा हैं?
बहुत ही खूबसूरत जगह पर घूमने जाने का।
लगभग लोग ये सपना अपने साथी, या दोस्तो के साथ देखना पसंद
करते हैं,
लेकिन मैं अकेले जाना चाहती थी, एक अनजान सा शहर, अजनबी
लोग, ना कोई पहचान ना कोई तकरार, बस खुद का खुद से रिश्ता।
तो, सुकून की तालाश में भागी मैं इस भीड़ भरी दुनिया से दूर,
जहा मेरा कोई ना हो, कोई पहचाने ना,
अजनबी चेहरों के बीच रह कर अजनबी दोस्तो के साथ सफर
गुजारूं,
तो, मैं इस हसीन सफर पर चल पड़ी,
आदत थी मेरी जब भी सफर पर चलती हूं बस गीत सुनना पसंद
करती हूं, तो इयर फोन लगा कर शांत सी खिड़की में बस नजारा
देखती रही
मेरे पास मै तीन लड़कियां भी बैठी थी, शायद वो भी दुनियां की
भीड़ से दूर आयी थी, रास्ते में अचानक भूख सी लगी मुझे,
जो खाना मैं खुद के लिए लाई थी, शायद मैं घर पर ही भूल गई थी,
तो वो लड़कियों ने मुझे खाना खाने के लिए पूछ लिए,
मैं भूख के मेरे बेशरम सी हो कर उनके साथ खाने लग गई,
खाना खाते खाते बातें होने लगी,
तो पता चला कि वो लखनऊ से हैं
और ट्रिप पर निकली हैं,
एक लड़की उनमें से बहुत बोलती थी, एक बस किताबो की दुनियां
में खोई सी रहती थी, और एक जो हर वक़्त खाना खाने में व्यस्त
रहती थी, अच्छी दोस्ती हो गई थी रास्ते में, बातें करते करते सफर
कब बीत गया कुछ पता नहीं चला,
तो जब हम अपनी मंजिल पर पहुंचे तो काफी रात हो चुकी थी,तो
सोना ही अच्छा समझा।
सुबह उठते ही में सुकून की तालाश में वो सूरज उगने का नजारा
देखने चली गई, वो नज़ारा देख मेरे चेहरे पर एक राहत सी आ गई,
वो राहत, भीड़ में भी एक चुप्पी की तरह थी,

उन दोस्तों के साथ पहाड़ों की सैर करने निकल गई, दो दिन क्या खूब गुज़रे,
ऐसा लग रहा था जैसे, मैंने अपनी ज़िन्दगी की सारी थकान उतार दी हो, और शांत समन्दर की तरह मन को भर दिया हो।

Amruta Thakare

Amruta Thakare is Passionate Writer. She is from Maharashtra. Amruta is an undergraduate student from Nashik University. She loves to speak truth and write by heart in the form of Poems, Shayari, One liners , Microtale. Her hobbies apart from writing includes Dancing, Singing, Anchoring, Reading books as well.
Instagram Handle @_nayisoch

खूबसूरत लम्हें, मेरा यादगार सफ़र"

सर्दियों के मौसम मे दिनांक १ जनवरी २०२०, मैं मेरे उपचरिक कार्य को खत्म करके एक सुनसान रास्तों से गुजर रही थी। मेरे मन मे कुछ अलग से विचार मेरी ही आवजों मे गूंज रहे थे,"शायद मैं अपनी व्यस्त भरी जिंदगी से थक चुकी हूँ, काश मैं एक खूबसूरत जगह पर अपने जिंदगी के कुछ यादगार लम्हें बना पाती"। ऐसे ही मन मे विचार करते हुए मैं अपने छात्रावास मे आ पहुँची। हर रोज की तरह अपने काम मे लगे रहना,जारी था। उसी दौरान मेरे फोन पर एक संदेश आया,

"आप सभी को सूचित किया जाता हैं की, ७ जनवरी 2020 ठीक सुबह ४.४५ को महाराष्ट्र के एक सुंदर सी जगह घूमने जा रहे हैं। धन्यवाद!

...आपकी शिक्षिका"

जैसे ही हम सभी उपचरिको ने वह संदेश पढ़ा, ख़ुशियों की धमाल सी मचने लगी, और मेरे मन मे "मेरा काश" पुरा हो रहा, यह चल रहा था। सभी उपचरिक् उस दिन के इंतज़ार मे खोय हुए थे। ख़ुशियों की लहर मेरे चहेरे पर चमक रही थी। रोज की तरह हम अपने उपचरिक कार्य के लिए निकल पड़े, पर इसबार एक खुशल सी चमक सभी के चहेरो पर झलक रही थी।

६ जनवरी २०२०, हम खुबसूरत लम्हों को यादगार पलों मे गुजारने की बातें कर रहे थे और हमे एक संदेश अपनी फोन मे आता हैं, "क्या आप सब टूर के लिए तैयार हो?, कल ठीक सुबह ४.४५ को तैयार रहिये, सभी को शुभ यात्रा!"यह संदेश पढ़कर सब अपनी तैयारी मे लगे थे। रात हुई, सबकी आँखें खूबसूरती लम्हों के इंतज़ार मे जागी थी। और मैं एक एक पलों को यादगार बनाने की योजना बना रही थी।

सुबह का वक़्त और मेरे मन मे ख्याल आया, "आखिर वह घड़ी आ गई, ७ जनवरी २०२०"। मैं उत्सुकता से जल्दबाजी मे तैयारी करते रही और देखा तो ठीक सुबह ४.४५ हमारे छात्रावास के बाहर हमारी बस खड़ी हुई थी। बस की ओर दोड़ते हुए मै विंडोव सीट पर बैठ गई और मैं अपना समान रखते हुए मैंने एक आवाज सुनी, "क्या आप सब तैयार हो?" सब उत्सुकता से शोर मचाते हुए, "हाँ ..." बस हमारी शुरू हो गई, और मैं चलती बस मे कैमरा मे खूबसूरत नज़ारे को कैद कर रही थी। वह लहराती हुई हवा जैसे मेरे बालों मे उलझ रही हो। कुछ समय बाद हम खूबसूरत जगह पर आ पहुँचे और मैंने एक बोर्ड पर लिखा था, "Amazing Place Khindsi" मैं बहुत ज्यादा उत्साहित थी। एक एक लम्हा जिंदगी मे यादगार बनाना चाहती थी। अलग सी वह जगह, कुछ खेल, वर्षा वाला नृत्य, नौका विहार, तैराकी, डिस्को डांस, इत्यादि सभी का आनंद लेने लगी। मेरी जिंदगी हाफ़ सेंचुरि की भी नही हुई है पर मानो मैंने फुल सेंचुरि के यादगार लम्हें, हसीन पल उस एक दिन मे गुजारे हो। ना कोई उपचरिक कार्य, ना कोई तनाव, बस वह "Amazing Place Khindsi" खूबसूरत और उत्साहिक जगह थी। असली मुस्कान, दिल की खुशी वह बरकरार रही थी। सब जानते है की, उपचरिक् लोगों को उत्साही जीवन जीने के लिए वक़्त नही रहता, पर जैसे ही मैं अपने व्यस्त जीवन मे लौटी उन लम्हों की याद मे व्यस्त जीवन जी रही हुँ। कोई तनाव या कोई थकावट सी हो,"खूबसूरत लम्हें, मेरा यादगार सफ़र" खिली हुई मुस्कुराहट मे बदल जाता हैं।

आज तस्वीरों मे कैद वह ख़ुशियाँ, वह उत्साहित जीवन की बातें मेरी कलम बया कर रही हैं।

Hina Patel

Hina Patel is accountant by profession. listening music is her passion. she is always love to create something new. she always ready to tackle with new world. She is love to traveling and watching movies. she love her family and any things can do it for her family.

Instagram Handle @hinapatel18

मेरा यादगार प्रवास - माउंट आबु- अंबाजी

मैंने वैसे तो बहुत जगह प्रवास किया हे लेकिन माउंट आबु- अंबाजी मेरा सबसे प्रिय स्थल है। हम लोग चार दिन के प्रवास पे दीवाली की छुट्टियो मे परिवार मित्र के साथ कार से गये थे। सबसे पहले अंबाजी गब्बर के दर्शन के लिए रात को ही घर से निकल गए धे। गब्बर हम ऊडन खटोले मे बैठ ओर मंदिर तक सिडया चठे। गब्बर की टोच पर मा अंबे के दर्शन कर बहुत आनंद आया। वहा की ठंडी हवा मन को प्रफुल्लित कर गई। वहा हमने दर्शन करने के बाद आराम किया मार्केट मै घूमे फिर हम माउंट आबु के लिए निकल गए ।। माउंट आयु का रास्ता डरवना और खुबसुरत हे। पेट मै गुदगुद करे वेस रास्ते हे । माउंट आबु मे हमने नखी लेक (तालाब)के पास होटल ली थी।। हमारे रुम की खिड़की से ठंडी है आ रही थी। हम लोग ने तालाब मे बोट भी चलाए ओर हाथ मे चाई की बनी मेहन्दी लगाई पर वो तालाब मे खेलते समय साफ हो गई। बहुत हो आई तब। तालाब मे बहुत सारी मछली थी ऊनको दाने डले ।। फिर हमने वह राजस्थानी कपडो मे फोटो खिचाई ओर वह खेल ओर होटल मे खाना खाया ।।

शाम को हम सनसेट पोईट गये। सूरज को आथमते हुए देखा वो बहुत सुन्दर दृश्य था ।। रात को वापस नखी तलाब के किनारे बैठ गए । वह मेन धोडेसवारी भी की धोडे को चने खिलाये ।। अगले दिन फिर हमने बाकी स्थल देखे। गुरुसिखर, देलवडा ना देर , वगेरे वह जैन मंदिर आतिसुदंर हे। माउंट आबू स्वर्ग जैसा खुबसूरत स्थल हे। बार बार जाने का मन कर राह हा। लोग को वह घुमने जाना चहिए। चारो दिशा जहाॅ नजर पोहचे वहा तक हरियाली , ऊंचे -

ऊंचे पाहड , ठंडी हवा ।। बादल तो इतने पास दिखे जैसे हाथ से छुले।
तो यह है मेरा यादगार सफर ।।

Kuber Sharma.

Grooming Poet. Poetry is his passion. He is serious about his passion. He wrote so many poetries. He wants to make his name in poetry.
Instagram Handle @Kuber.58

विदेश की सैर पहली बार करी,
पहली बार कहीं बाहर गया था,
चढ़ा ही था साल 2020 शुरुआत में ही मैं दुबई गया था,
अलग ही था नज़ारा वहाँ का कुछ बड़ी बड़ी इमारते थीं,
मन में एक अलग ही सुकून था जब मेरी आँखें उन इमारतों को
निहारती थी,

बह गया था समुंद्र के ख्वाब में जहाँ बिल्कुल शांति थी,
शांत ज़िन्दगी साफ सड़के ज़िन्दगी जीने का अंदाज़ अलग,
बस गया था मेरा दिल वहीं पर और मेरे ख्वाब भी थे कुछ अलग,
देख रहा था दुबई का माहौल जैसे हो दुनिया से अलग,
सच में लगा मुझे जैसे मैं हूँ पूरी दुनिया से अलग ।

Neeti Gupta

Neeti Gupta, born and raised in Punjab, is a Homemaker and an enthusiastic writer as well She is part of various writing communities, events and anthologies. Her writings are inspired by mythology, philosphy and real life situations. Her hobbies, apart from writing includes cooking, drawing and singing as well. Her family is most dearest to her.

यात्रा

यात्रा एक ऐसी सुन्दर और
सुखद अनुभूति है
जो तन को ही नहीं सबके
मन को तृप्त करती है
यात्रा के प्रति सम्मोहन
इतना गहरा होता है
थका इंसान घूम फिर कर
आराम महसूस करता है
भाग दौड़ वाली ज़िन्दगी में
जहाँ ज़िम्मेदारियां हैं इतनी
मन उत्साहित हो जाता है
घूम आने से कहीं
दोस्तों और परिवार के साथ यात्रा
में यादगार पल बनते हैं
वही पल काम की थकावट में
हमें मुस्कुराहट देते हैं
मेरी पसंदीदा यात्रा मेरे परिवार
के साथ ही जाना है
छुट्टी मिल जाए जब काम से
तो बस घूमना घूमाना है
मनाली, शिमला या मंसूरी
कोई भी जगह हो
घूमना बड़ा अच्छा लगता है
मौसम जब सुहाना हो
मकलोड़ गंज का खाना
और पेय बड़े ही याद आते हैं
कार की गति धीमी
और संगीत भी धीमा बजे

घर से तैयार पकवान हम
कार में ही खाते हैं
तारीफ करते हैं सब मेरी
जब सबमें बांटे जाते हैं
रास्ते में कारों में सबकी होती
रहती है अदला-बदली
मैं जाती हूं अपने भाई की कार में
और मेरी कार में और कोई
रोक कर गाडियाँ अपनी
पीते हैं चाय या ठण्डा
खाते हैं पीज़ा, समोसा
या हो जो मन का
ये दिन सारा साल
आते हैं बहुत याद हमें
देखतें हैं कई बार
खींची हुई तस्वीरें
काश जल्दी आ जाए वो समय
जब जाना हो अगली बार
सभी को रहता है इंतज़ार

Padma Srivastava

She is from Varanasi. She is pursuing graduation from B. H. U . She is a student of Archaeology with it she is also a good writer She writes poem since 8th standard . She is Fond of singing and writing and composing poetry. She has been co _author of 4+anthologies except it
Instagram Handle @Perfectsriva_quotes

बड़े अरसे हो गए हैं,,,
मैं कुछ वादियों से मिलना चाहती हूं
जहां हो पर्वतमालाएं कई,,,
जहां अनेकों नदियों का राज्य हो
दबी हो कई पुरातात्विक बातें
हर चित्रकारी में कोई बात हो
सुनो ना! मैं इटली जाना चाहती हूँ।
सुना है भारत की कई चीजें
गिरवी रखीं हैं वहां पे....
एक दफ़ा उनसे मुलाकात करके
खुद सुकून पाना चाहती हूं।
ज़रा भारत के विरासत से तो मिलूं
देखूँ उनमें ऐसी ख़ासियत क्या थी
उठाकर ले गए शानो-शौकत हमारी
ऐसी उनमें काबिलियत क्या थी
उन अपने देश के यादों से
उन नदियों, उन शहर की हर हवाओं से
मैं कुछ बातें करना चाहती हूं
सुनो ना! मैं इटली जाना चाहती हूं।
कहते हैं.. बड़ा प्राचीन शहर है
प्राचीन विश्व की सभ्यता का नगर है
वहां की इमारतें,, वहां की संस्कृति
सबसे थोड़ा रू-ब-रू होना चाहती हूं
सुनो ना! मैं इटली जाना चाहती हूँ।
कोई भी जगह नज़रों से मेरे न बच पाए
जो खुद में ,,,
सदियों पुराना इतिहास छिपाए रखती है
जानना हैं ज़रा मुझे भी तो
वो कितनी सभ्यताओं का राज़ दबाए रखती है
उस ऐतिहासिक जगह पर
मुझे भी एक बार घूमना है।

अपने देश की विरासत को
अपने होठों से चूमना है ।
सुनो ना! मुझे भी इटली चलना है।।

Priyanka Khunt

She is priyanka khunt from Rajkot, Gujarat.she have completed master of social work.and you can read my write ups you will definitely feel
The pen is my palm,
And the text is my destiny ...!
Instagram Handle @different_dil_dude

रास्ते की पेहचान

कोई भी जगह उनके रास्ते की,
वजह से अच्छी लगती हैं..!
क्योंकि,हम सफ़र में सोचते है
क्या करना हैं..? कहाँ कहाँ धुमेंगे.?
कब मिलना हैं..?बात क्या करेंगे..?
वहां की सबसे अच्छी जगह कोनसी हैं..?
क्या खाओगे .? क्या पहनना हैं..?
ये सब हम रास्ते मे ही सोंचते हैं..!
और सोच से ही हम इतना खुश होते हैं..!
कि बात ही मत पूछो..!
इससे अच्छा मुझें रास्ते में खिड़की के बहार देखना..!
खुल्ली हवा को सांसो में भरना..!
आँखे बंध करके पंखिओ की आवाज़ सुनना..!
वृक्षों का हरा-भरा होना..! गीत गाना और सुनना..!
आकाश में देख के बातें करना..!
पहोचने के बाद ख़ूब सारी मस्ती करना..!
वापस आते समय फ़िर से सोचना..!
क्या क्या किया..! सारी बातें याद करना..!
फ़िर से अपने ही धुन में खो जाना मुझे अच्छा लगता हैं..!

Sahina Ghugha

Sahina Ghugha is 20 year old girl. She is from Jamnagar city of Gujarat. She is student of B.com at Saurashtra university Rajkot and state level winner in poetry competition 2017. Instagram Handle @Itz_sahina_write

कुछ खास मज़ा है इस सफर का
कुछ अलग ही अहेसास है।
न जाने कितने दिनों बाद
देखी गई अलग दुनिया है।

हवाएं लहराती जुल्फों के संग
दौड़ रहा नया रक्त अंग अंग।
खो जाने को जी चाहे इन वादियों में
रहे लू मैं इस जगह बना के सुरंग।

बाते करू इन बहेते झरनों से
बतियाऊ पक्षिओ के कलरव से।
ओढ़ लू चादर तारों भरे आसमां की
रहे जाऊ इन पहाड़ों के आरव में।

ये अहेसास है जूनागढ़ के आंगन का
गिरनार पर्वत और सिंह के सासण का।

Sarabjot Purba

Sarabjot Purba lives in Kotkapura, Punjab. He wrote a poem for the first time when he was in class XI. After this While studying E.T.T., he started writing poems as well as essays and stories. He has given the thoughts of his mind in the form of a book. Whose name is 'Kuz Vichar'. He also wrote some pages related to E.T.T. College time. He has written something on every subject. He often writes on issues of society. He mostly use Punjabi language. Instagram Handle @purba_poetry

मनाली की यात्रा

एक बार की बात सुनाता हूँ,
जब मैं गया था मनाली।
दिन में होती है हलचल,
रोशन होती है रात काली।
दूर-दूर से लोग आते है,
देखने प्राकृति के यह रंग।
ऊँचे-ऊँचे पर्वत देखकर,
सभी लोग हो जाते दंग।
चारो ओर ही है हरियाली,
जिससे मन खुश होता है।
यहाँ तो कोई शोर भी नहीं,
आदमी आराम से सोता है।
पक्षीयो की चहचहाहट से,
सच में मन खिल जाता है।
सुनते ही उनकी मधुर ध्वनि,
सिर दर्द भी भाग जाता है।
काम की परेशानी होती नहीं,
मन तो यहीं खो जाता है।
मनाली जो एक बार आऐ,
बस मनाली का हो जाता है।

Sarvesh Upadhyay

Sarvesh Upadhyay the one who pens down his thoughts by writing poetry. He has great interest in reading books as well as listening music and gazals and with this enthusiasm he still continues his poetry. Sarvesh is currently focusing on his career and pursuing BAMS from Bhopal. He has contributed in many anthologies and now he has compiled 3 books. Instagram Handle @originalwrites

मन की धारणा

जिंदगी में कुछ चीज़े बिना कुछ ज्यादा सोचे हो जाती है, कुछ समय पहले की बात है, कॉलेज से हमे दो दिन की छुट्टी मिली थी, पहले तो कुछ किसी ने सोचा भी नहीं था, अचानक रात को 10 बजे एक दोस्त बोलता है, चलो उज्जैन चलते है, 11 बजे तक हम चारो तैयार, लेकिन अब जाना जनरल डब्बे में था, अब जनरल डब्बे का नाम सुन के मेरे हाथ पैर फूलने लगते थे, उन्होंने कहा इसी से चलना पड़ेगा और कुछ नहीं है, अब जनरल डब्बे में इतनी भीड़ केसे क्या होगा, ये सोचते हुए 2 बजे हम स्टेशन के लिए निकले, ट्रेन थी, 3:50 की, हम लोग स्टेशन पोहचे टिकट लेने के लिए जैसे ही टिकट वाले को जगाया उसका ऐसा रिएक्शन मानो बोल रहा हो इतनी रात में सफर करते क्यू हो, स्टेशन में ज्यादा लोग थे नहीं, कुछ मुंह पे मच्छर मारते हुए बैठे थे, कुछ अपनी बाबू को मना रहे थे, और कुछ हम जैसे बार बार घड़ी, और प्लेटफॉर्म में दोनों तरफ देख रहे थे कहीं से तो कोई ट्रेन आओ, मुझे याद है, एक अंकल का रिजर्वेशन ए.सी डब्बे में था, वो बिचारे दरवाजा बजा बजा के परेशान की कोई तो खोल दो, ट्रेन जाने को हुई तब जा के एक की नींद खुली तब उसने दरवाजा खोला, अंकल के गुस्से का स्तर समझ आ रहा था, जिस ट्रेन से हमें जाना था उसकी अनाउंसमेंट हुआ, मेरे मन में एक ही ख्याल आया ये दोस्त आज जान ले लेंगे उस भीड़ में, ट्रेन अ॰ई हम आखिरी डब्बे में जैसा मैने सोचा था, हां बैसा ही था, डब्बे के दरवाजे तक लोग खड़े थे, मेरा जैसे तैसे अंदर पहुंचे, भाईसाब गर्दन टेडी करने तक की जगह नहीं थी, चारो दोस्त कुंभ के मेले की तरह बिछड़ गए, मैने जैसे तैसे कर के फोन लगाया एक को उसने बताया कि बाकी दो दूसरे डब्बे में चड़ गए, अगले स्टेशन में इसमें आ जाएंगे, 3 की सीट में 5 बैठे थे, की एक अंकल बोले बेटा तुम कब

तक खड़े रहोगे, ए खिसको रे लड़के को बैठने दो, ऐसा उन्होंने बगल वाले को बोला, और वो चुप चाप खिसक गए, अब 3 की सीट में 6 लोग, अक्सर समय निकालने को लोग पड़ोस वाले से व बात करने लगते है, तो ऐसे बात शुरू हुई, धीरे धीरे बाकी 4 भी जाग गए और सामने की सीट वाले भी, मैने किसी की बहू ऐसी है से लेके सास तक, सारे रिश्तेदार और एक के फलाने का लड़का उसके चाचा के जो ससुर है, उनके भाई का लड़का भी भोपाल से पढ रहा है, अब ये सब पता था मुझे, काफी घरवालों जैसा एहसास था, ये किस्सा यही ख़तम करना होगा लिमिट के कारण, जारी रखेंगे फिर कभी,

बस इतना समझा में दिल में जगह हो तो सीट में व जगह बिना मिल जाती है, वो 4-5 घंटे पता नहीं केसे निकल गए, बिना फोन चलाए, जैसा सोचा था, उससे अलग एक अनोखा सफर

Shadab Jahan

She is "SHADAB JAHAN" from Bhopal Madhya Pradesh. She is working under the department of women and child development. She has been active in the field of writing for a long time. She is an excellent cook as well as skilled in painting and artistry. She is also a good orator. She is adept at embellishing her emotions with words and pearls, and remains devoted to her work. Her hobbies are painting, writing, crafts and art work, stitching, cooking etc etc. She specializes in many tasks, so her loved ones call her an all-rounder.

वो महिला कुली (कहानी)

ज़िन्दगी संघर्ष का दूसरा नाम है ये तो कई बार सुना है लेकिन जो संघर्ष कर विजय प्राप्त करे वही तो वास्तव मे विजेता है कुछ ऐसा ही जीवन मे देखने को मिला साथ ही स्त्री जीवन के संघर्ष और एक स्त्री के बुलंद हौसलो से पहचान भी हुई। बात ज़्यादा पुरानी तो नहीं पर साल दो साल पहले की रही होगी. जब आगरा केंट स्टेशन पर एक महिला कुली को देखा। उसके हाथ पर बिल्ला बंधा हुआ था सावला चेहरा बड़ी बड़ी आँखे चेहरे पर चमक थी कुछ चालीस-पेतालीस साल उम्र रही होगी उसकी । बालो का जूढ़ा बनाए तोलीया कंधे पर डाले हुए वह मर्दों के से स्टाइल में खड़ी थी हम आश्चर्य से उसे देखने लगे थोड़ी हैरानी हुई औरत और कुली ..? बिजली जैसी तेजी से उसने भारी-भारी सूटकेस बैग और थैले गाडी पर रख दिए और उन्हें रस्सी से बाँध दिया और तेज कदमो से गाडी को धकाती आगे-आगे चलने लगी मेरी माँ ने उस से बाते शुरू की उसने अपना नाम मनोरमा बताया - "तुम औरत होकर कुली का काम करती हो " वह हँस कर थोड़ा मजाकिया लहजे में बोली - "हाँ बाई जी ज़िन्दगी का बोझ ढ़ोते-ढोते आदत पड़ गई " कुछ ही देर मे हम प्लेटफार्म पर आ गए थे माँ ने उससे पूछा -"तुम्हारा पति क्या करता है?" बाई जी मै तो सालो से नहीं जानती पति क्या होता है ? "क्यों तुम्हारा पति नहीं है क्या ?" माँ ने खोजती नज़रो से पूछा - "छोटे- छोटे बच्चे थे जब छोड़ के भाग गया मुझे,बेवड़ा कही का दारुखोर था साला बच्चों को पालने के लिए तब से ये काम कर रही हूं बाई जी "छोटे- छोटे बच्चे है तुम्हारे " मेरी माँ ने पूछा - "नहीं एक बेटा बड़ा है कॉलेज पड़ता है,एक छोटा है स्कूल जाता है । बड़ा बेटा ट्यूशन भी पढाता है और खाली समय मे मुझे भी पढाता है अपने जीवन के संघर्ष की कहानी वो माँ को सुना रही थी उसने बताया छोटी उम्र मे उसकी शादी हो गई थी पढ़-लिख नहीं पाई बाप शराबी था घर के हालात ख़राब थे जल्दी जल्दी दो बच्चे हो गए | और न जाने क्या क्या बताती रही थी वो । मै चुपचाप दिलचस्पी से

उनका वार्तालाप सुनती रही वह औरत संघर्ष की प्रतिमूर्ति प्रतीत हो रही थी तभी गाड़ी प्लेटफार्म पर आ कर रुकी यात्री तेज़ी से दौडे कुछ को चढ़ने की जल्दी थी कुछ को उतरने की कुछ दो-तीन मिनट मे उसने तेज़ी से पूरा सामान डिब्बे के अंदर रख दिया । पापा ने उसे उसकी मेहनत के रूपये अदा कर दिए थे। सिग्नल हो चुका था सबको सलाम करती वह गाड़ी से तेज़ी से उतर गई और मै सोचने लगी की स्त्री आज भी अबला भी है और सबला भी पर यह इस बात पर निर्भर करता है कि वह किस रूप मे खुद को देखना चाहती है गाड़ी धीरे- धीरे बढ़ने लगी थी सब बातो मे खो गए थे लेकिन मेरा ध्यान अब भी पीछे ही था मेरे मानस पटल पर मनोरमा चलचित्र की भाँति चल रही थी एक स्त्री होने के नाते मुझे उससे हमदर्दी सी हो गई थी मै बाहर का सुहावना नज़ारा देख रही थी पर कही अंदर मेरा मन बैचेन सा था।

Sheikh Mohammad Junaid

He is "SHEIKH MOHAMMAD JUNAID" from Bhopal Madhya Pradesh. He is a student of b.ed and he is also an accountant. He has been active in the field of writing for the last 3 years. He have been active on "YOUR QUOTE" since may 2020 and have written many ghazals on it. Mostly he write on love but sometimes his thoughts are also focused on other subjects. When his mood is at a different level, it often creates poetry. He has the ability to put his emotions into words.Whenever he writes something, he is dedicated to someone.

Email - mohammadjunaid078603@gmail.com

अभद्रता (कहानी)

समीर इंदौर की एक मल्टीनेशनल कंपनी मे मैनेजर के पद पर पदस्थ है। कई दिनों बाद समीर को उसके ऑफिस से अवकाश मिला तो समीर अपने घर जा रहा है। समीर रायसेन जिले का रहने वाला है। समीर के मन मे कई विचार चल रहे थे। बस के ड्राइवर ने ब्रेक लगाया तो समीर का ध्यान भंग हुआ। पास बैठे यात्री से समीर ने पूछा तो पता चला कि भोपाल बस स्टॉप आ चुका है।

बस के रुकते ही एक वृद्ध महिला बस मे सवार हुई। बस कुछ ही आगे बड़ी होगी कि बस के कंडक्टर ने यात्रीयों का टिकट काटना शुरू किया। जब कंडक्टर उस वृद्ध महिला के पास पंहुचा तो उस महिला ने हाथ जोड़ते हुए बड़ी ही विनम्रता के साथ कंडक्टर से कहा कि -" बेटा मुझे रायसेन तक जाना है, वहाँ मेरे बेटे का एक्सीडेंट हो गया है वह सरकारी अस्पताल मे भर्ती है, मेरे पास इतने रूपये नहीं है कि मै बस का टिकट खरीद सकूँ मेरी तुमसे हाथ जोड़कर विनती है कि मै बस के एक कोने मे नीचे बैठे-बैठे चली जाऊँगी सीट पर नहीं बैठूंगी, मेरा टिकट मत काटो।"

यह सुनते ही कंडक्टर उस महिला से अभद्रता करने लगा। उसने बस के ड्राइवर से कहा - "बस रोको इस बुढ़िया को नीचे उतारो।"

कंडक्टर द्वारा अभद्रता किए जाने पर समीर खामोश नहीं रहा। समीर ने उस कंडक्टर से कहा -" इनकी जगह अगर तुम्हारी माँ होती तब भी तुम उनके साथ ऐसे ही बर्ताव करते क्या ? तुम्हे शर्म नहीं आती यह अपनी मजबूरी बता रही है और तुम इनकी परेशानी समझने के लिए तैयार ही नहीं हो कम-से-कम इनकी उम्र का ही लिहाज़ कर लो।"

कंडक्टर ने कहा-" तुम जानते भी हो भोपाल से रायसेन का किराया 80 रूपये है मै अपने 80 रूपये का नुकसान क्यों करू?"

समीर ने कहा -" 80 रूपये इनके सम्मान से बढ़कर है क्या? तुम्हारे लिए होंगे मेरे लिए नहीं। मै इनके बेटे के समान हूं और मेरी माँ से अभद्रता करने वाले का मै मुँह भी तोड़ सकता हूं लेकिन मै ऐसा करूंगा नहीं।"

इतना कहकर समीर ने 100 रूपये का नोट कंडक्टर की ओर बढ़ाते हुए उस महिला का टिकट बनाने को कहा। कंडक्टर ने 80 रूपये काटते हुए बाकी बचे 20 रूपये और टिकट समीर को थमा दिए। समीर ने सम्मानपूर्वक उस महिला से सीट पर बैठने का आग्रह किया। और कहा-" अम्मा आपको नीचे बैठकर जाने की कोई ज़रूरत नहीं है।" वह महिला आँखों मे आंसू लिए और हाथ जोड़ते हुए मानो समीर का धन्यवाद ! कर रही थी।

Shipra S Gupta

Shipra is the Founder of www.hijindgi.com .She has done teaching almost a decade. She is a blogger, writer and poetess. Her favourite job is the one now she is doing full time writing. She lives in Delhi NCR with her husband and children.

If you want to know more about her kindly visit her website www.hijindgi.com

Instagram Handle @shipra027

बचपन का यादगार लम्हा

बचपन के लम्हें हमेशा दिल में एक याद बन कर रहते है। ऐसा ही एक लम्हा मेरी जिंदगी में भी है।

हम सब भाई बहन जब पापा मम्मी के साथ शिमला घूमने गए थे। हमारी गर्मियों की छुट्टियां चल रही थी तो हमने पापा से कहा की इस बार हमें भी कही ऐसी जगह जाना है जहा पर पहाड़ हो। मम्मी की एक सहेली थी जिनका नाम राज ऑन्टी था। उन्होंने मम्मी के साथ मिलकर कार्यक्रम बनाया की शिमला घूमने चलो। हम भी तुम सभी के साथ चलेंगे।

हम दिल्ली से शिमला के लिए टैक्सी में गए। रास्ते भर हम भाई बहन बहुत खुश थे। एक दूसरे के साथ हँसी मजाक करते हुए कब हम पानीपत, करनाल होते शिमला पहुँच गए पता ही नहीं चला।

वहाँ पहुँच कर हम एपल ट्री नाम के होटल में रुके। उस होटल की रौनक देखते ही बनती थी। वो होटल बहुत सुंदर था। हम लिफ्ट को देख कर इतने खुश थे की बार बार बहाने से कभी ऊपर की मंजिल पर जाते तो कभी नीचे की। उसके बाद हम सब खाना खाकर सो गए।

सुबह उठते ही हम सब तैयार होकर जाखू मंदिर के लिए जाने को होटल से निकले। उस समय जाखू मंदिर के लिए पैदल ही जाना होता था। ऑन्टी बोली मैं तो नहीं चढ़ाई कर सकती, तुम लोग जाओ।

मुझे ऑन्टी का नीचे रहना मंजूर नही था। मैंने कहा ऑन्टी आप हमारे साथ चलो, थोड़ी हिम्मत तो करो। ऑन्टी को मेरे ऐसा कहते ही चढ़ाई का हौसला मिला और उन्होंने चलने की ठान ली।

दरसल ऑन्टी मोटी होने की वजह से पहले घबरा रही थी। मेरे साथ बातें करते- करते वो कब ऊपर तक की चढ़ाई चढ़ गई, उन्हे भी पता नहीं चला। उपर जाकर बोली शिप्रा तू मुझे यहाँ तक ले आई। मैं तो कभी अकेले नहीं आ पाती।

उसके बाद हमने मंदिर में दर्शन किए। वहाँ पर बहुत सारे बंदर भी थे। हम सभी ने बंदरों को केले खिलाए थे। फिर हम नीचे वापस आ

117

गए। शाम को पापा, मम्मी, अंकल, ऑन्टी और हम सब भाई, बहन माल रोड घूमने गए। वहाँ इतना अच्छा नजारा था की मैं वहां की वादियों मे खो सी गई। उस समय मेरी उम्र यही कोई बारह साल की होगी। फिर माल रोड की वो सुंदरता आज तक मेरे दिल में ज्यों की त्यों है।

उस रात हम सभी ने मिलकर अंताक्षरी खेली। रात का खाना खाया और सो गए।

सुबह होते ही हम सब वापस दिल्ली के लिए निकल गए। आज पापा, मम्मी, ऑन्टी हमारे बीच नहीं है। भगवान ने उन्हें अपने पास बुला लिया पर बचपन की ये यात्रा आज भी मेरे मानस पटल पर एक याद की तरह अंकित है।

Shivika Sharma

Shivika Sharma is a writer. She is a college student. She live in kawardha Chhattisgarh. She loves to write poems, quotes & shayaris etc.She used yourquote app for presenting her views.
Instagram handle @shivika1108

एक यादगार पल

ये उस समय की बात है,
जब हम गये थे एक मंदिर।
हैं वो दैवी मां का मंदिर,
नाम है जतमई-घटारानी
बहुत ही अनोखा मंदिर है,
खुबसूरती की पावन भूमि हैं।
दैवी मां की तो प्रतिमा,
बेहद ही मनमोहनी हैं।।
अत्यधिक सुंदर प्राकृतिक से भरा,
हैं वो पर्यटन स्थल।
अनेकों श्रद्धालूओं आते हैं वहां,
करने दैवी मां के दर्शन।।
गये थे सपरिवार सहित हम,
दैवी मां के दर्शन करने को।
बहुत सुंदर यादगार पल है,
अब हम याद करते हैं तो।।

एक प्यारा सफर

एक ऐसा सफर,
जो सबसे ज्यादा यादगार हैं।
वो जब हम अपने स्कूल के,
दोस्तों के साथ पिकनिक पर गए थे।।
जाते-जाते वक्त हम सब,
गाना गाते हुए गये थे।
पहुंचने के बाद हम,
बहुत ही ज्यादा मस्ती किये थे।।
रायपुर में स्थित एम-एम-फनसीटी हैं,
जहां हम गये थे।
पानी के साथ हम वहां,
बहुत ही ज्यादा खेले थे।।
हम जब वापस हुए थे,
तो बहुत सारे यादें साथ लाए थे।
और बहुत ही ज्यादा मस्ती,
हम वहां किये थे।।

बहुत ही ज्यादा मज़ा आया था,
वो स्कूल के दोस्तों के साथ।
वो लम्हा हमारा एक प्यारा सा सफर है,
जो कभी भुलाया नहीं जाता हैं।।

Shresth Bhargava (Yash)

Shresth Bhargava (Yash), is an emerging writer,author as well as compiler from The city of Love, The city of Taj AGRA.In his point of view , 'we can bring positive changes in the lives of peoples as well as we can ir-radicate social-evil's from our community by the help of our writings'.Apart from his writtings ,he is also a CA Aspirant ,His aim of life is to help mankind and bring positive changes in the lives of his countrymen .He has won various certificates in various competitions,He is always there for help of peoples in need .He is nature loving person,He is a devotee of Lord Shiva .He respect the ones who respects him and himself .He is verey friendly person,for him his family and friends is his lifeline Intagram Handle @yashbhargava2000

यह बहुत समय पहले था जब मोबाइल फोन कुछ विशेषाधिकार प्राप्त लोगों के लिए थे। मैं आगरा से जयपुर जा रहा था और वह मेरे सामने बैठी थी। यह पहली नजर का प्यार था। हमने संगीत और पुस्तकों में रुचि साझा की। अकेले और अकेले यात्रा करते हुए, मुझे लगता है कि हम एक-दूसरे से मिलना चाहते थे। थोड़ी देर के बाद, हमने हाथ पकड़े और घंटों बात की। अंत में, हम जयपुर पहुँचे और एक दूसरे को आंसू अलविदा बोली। और अचानक मुझे एहसास हुआ, मैंने कभी उसका नाम नहीं पूछा। हमने कभी भी मार्ग नहीं जोड़े या पार किए। मैं हमेशा उसे अपने जीवन के सबसे पहले प्यार के रूप में याद करता हूं।

एक बार ट्रेन में एक अजनबी से मिला और उससे लगभग 2 घंटे बात की। बाद में, उसने मुझे अपना नंबर दिया और ट्रेन से उतर गई। हमने अगले 5 साल तक संपर्क बनाए रखा है। लेकिन चूंकि लंबी दूरी के रिश्ते कभी काम नहीं करते, इसलिए हमने इसे बंद कर दिया। लेकिन मुझे हमेशा आश्चर्य होता है, ट्रेन यात्रा की पेशकश करने वाली गंभीरता - और कुछ नहीं हो सकती। यह अद्भुत है कि यह कैसे चिरस्थायी संबंधों का निर्माण कर सकता है।

Shruti Mahajan

You are Shruti Mahajan, you are from commerce background, and you are from Indore, but your heart is also in poetry and photography, painting. You are a housewife, and so far your poetry has come in three of my books, titled An Ek Goonj and Titli, Lesson To Remember. And you will want to continue working in the same way. Hope you will like these poems.

Instagram Handle @arts_and_poetrys @mahajanshruti.106

उस सफर की क्या बात करू जिसमे मेरा खाब न हो उस जिगर की क्या बात कर जिसमे मेरा हर एक सपना न हो।

उड़ते हुए पक्षी की तरह उड़ना है। -स्काई डाइविंग

उन वादियों में जाना है जहाँ चारो और पहाड़ियों की वादी हो-लद्दाख

उस नीले आस्मां के नीचे नीला समंदर हो-बाली

इसी तरह के खाब है कुछ मेरे ।

लोग भागते है सफलता के पीछे ।पर मुझे भागना है लोकप्रियता के पीछे कम लोग समझ पाते है सपना क्या है असली हक़ीक़क़त में खुद ही की जुबान है।चाहे हो कलम की बात या चित्रकारी या फोटोग्राफी की खुद का आयाम बनाना है।आज हूं सह लेखक पर कल मुझे खुद लेखिका बनना है।उस पुस्तक में जिंगदी की खूबसूरती को उतारना है।

जो सपने देखे है ।उन लोगो ने उन्हें उभारना है।एक सह लेखिका की कहानी है अभी ये सपनो की ।जिसे लेखिका बनकर असलियत में उतारना है। नासमझ नहीं होते वो लोग भी जो सपने नहीं देखते उनसे जाके पूछो जो झोपड़ियों में हर रोज नए सपने बुनते है।रही चादर छोटी तो क्या मगर दिल में खाब तो बुनते है।सपना होता ही है।हर एक का तभी तो बुनते है।

"कभी कभी जिंदगी छोटी पड़ जाती है।पर सपने पूरे नही हो पाते ।आस न छोड़ो ऐ हमसफ़र तलाश में भी सपने पूरे होते है।"

महाबलेश्वर

उम्दा वादिया ,हरियाली थी ठंडी हवा,मुसकुराहट ही थी।
प्रकृति को इतनी नज़दगी से देखा ।जिसमे स्ट्राबेरी के पेड़ और गुलाब की क्यारियां ही थी। उचाई को देख जाना हवा का अहसास क्या है वादिया इतनी खूबसूरत ठड के दिन की बात थी। औस ज्यादा खूबसूरत थी और उसपर धीमी बारिश खुशनुमा थी। 4 दिन गुजारे थे उन वादियों में साथ क्यों की पुणे के नज़दीक लवासा की भी तैयारी थी वहाँ का मौसम कुछ और पहाड़ो के बीच बस्ती सवारी थी पहाड़ो पे बस्ती उसकी क्या तारीफ करू वो भी एक कहानी थी।नीला आसमान पूल से नदी प्यारी थी । 4 दिन की छुट्टी में ही प्रकृति को देखा क्या कहूं ।अब आगे के सपनो की तैयारी थी ।अब जाना है लद्दाक बाली। सपने है जारी आगे भी है तैयारी बस इतनी ही अभी सफर की बारी थी।
"सपने हर कोई देखता है।सफर जारी है जिंदगी है साहब पर उम्मीदों की तैयारी है बस इतनी कहानी हैं।सफर है जिंदगी में तो खुशहाल जिंदगानी है।"

Tanishka Srivastava

She is Tanishka Srivastava. She is from Ayodhya, प्रभू श्री राम की नगरी I She has been writing since 10th standard. She scribbed some words, She got to know herself as a writer. Over the last 2 years, writing became her passion but more than that a medium to express our feelings, emotions and her innervoice. She started penning down her every motion be it Happiness, anger, love, hate, or disappointment. She consider pen, the best companion and hence through her writing she want to contribute in the making of this new era. Instagram Handle @ nature_lover_tanishka

सौभाग्य : सैर - ए - अवध

कभी मिलना अयोध्या की गलियों में , तुम्हारे साथ पूरा अवध घूमना है मुझे !!
नदियों की खूबसूरती को जी भर कर जिया है हमनें, तुम्हारी आंखों में शिल्प सौंदर्य देखना है मुझे !!
खुशनुमा शामें तो कई देखी है, तुम्हारे साथ सरयू आरती देखनी है मुझे !!
चिलकती धूप के किस्सों से भरी है अयोध्या अपनी, तुम्हारे साथ प्रकृति की शीतलता देखनी है मुझे !!

कभी मिलना अयोध्या की गलियों में, तुम्हारे साथ पूरा अवध घूमना है मुझे!!
चौक घंटाघर के शोर से जन्मों का नाता है , तुम्हारे साथ मिलिट्री मंदिर की शांति देखनी है मुझे!!
बिग बाज़ार की चकाचौंद में गुम से नज़र आए हम, तुम्हारे साथ बृहस्पति बाज़ार की रौनक देखनी है मुझे !!
प्रदूषित वातावरण में डूबी है ज़िन्दगी अपनी , तुम्हारे साथ कनक भवन की शुद्धता देखनी है मुझे !!

कभी मिलना अयोध्या की गलियों में, तुम्हारे साथ पूरा अवध घूमना है मुझे !!
यूं तो हमारी यारी में चर्चे मशहूर रहे हैं काफ़ी, ख़ैर तुमसे वही किस्से दोबारा सुनना है मुझे !!
अवंतिका में बिताए हर लम्हों को एक हसीं सदी सा जिया हमने , तुम्हारे साथ गलियों के जायकों से वाक़िफ होना है मुझे !!

कभी मिलना अयोध्या की गलियों में, तुम्हारे साथ पूरा अवध घूमना है मुझे !!

जाने माने रास्तों पर बेधड़क सैर हुई अपनी , तुम्हारे साथ अनजान रास्तों पर बेफ़िक्री से घूमना है मुझे !!

ज़माने की बंदिशों में तैरते नज़र आए हम , तुम्हारे साथ इन खूबसूरत वादियों में डूब जाना है मुझे !!

वाक़िफ तो तुम भी हो, भीड़ बहुत है अयोध्या की गलियों में, इसी भीड़ में तुम्हारा बचपन जीना है मुझे !!

कभी मिलना अयोध्या की गलियों में, तुम्हारे साथ पूरा अवध घूमना है मुझे !!

Vipul Sune

He is biotechnologist as well as writer , he has published his 3 books , he has published 100+ content stories and poetries on pratilipi app , u can go and read that content has being more popular . He has more than 5lakh reader at he owned a identity as a writer at age of 20 , he has his own visiting card given by pratilipi ...He is passionate and ambious person who always be in his world of dreams ....The bunny kinda a guy in yjhd who never want to stop
Instagram Handle @Vipulsune2126

हमारे बर्थडे के दिन हम पाताळेश्वर मंदिर गये थे दोस्त के साथ ,
नाम अलग है ना

उसका मतलब है पाणी के अंदर रेहणे वाले भगवान का मंदिर
,यानि के खुद्द शिव जी ..

सरल मंदिर है पर उसकी सरलता और ऐतिहासिक ता ही दिल जित
लेती है .

ये मंदिर जँगली महाराज रोड पर है जो की शिवाजी नगर , पुणे से
थोडा ही दूरी पर है ,

ये मंदिर पांडवो ने उनके आराम के लिये बनाया था ऐसा कहा जाता
है .

ये मंदिर रोड के लेवल से थोडा नीचे है , जाते ही एक गोलाकार
दगड से बना हुआ छत है जिसे नंदी मंडप कहा जात है . और उस
मंडप मे नंदी स्थापित है . उसके ठीक सामने शिव लिंग है .

वहा का तापमान बाहरी तापमान से बिलकुल कम और शांत है ,
अगर आप शांतिप्रिय व्यक्ती है तो ये मंदिर आपके लिये ही है , इस
मंदिर मे आने के बाद आपको बिलकुल भी इहसास नाही होगा के
आप पुणे जैसे मेट्रो सिटी मे है , ना कोई शोर ना कोई पोल्युशन

मैने पुरा मंदिर आपको अभिभी नही दिखाया है ,ताकी आप खुद्द
वहा जाऐंगे तो आप और कूछ अलग भी देखने को मिले ,

इस मंदिर को आप पढ या इंटरनेट पर देख कर नही सिर्फ वहा
जाकर ही उसकी वैशिष्ट्य की अनुभूती ले सकते है..

तो एक बार अवश्य जाये आपको यहा जाकर ना मनशांती और
सुकून जो मिलेगा वो आप भी बया नही कर पाएंगे

मंजिल मिलेगी गुम हो कर ही सही , गुम तो वो है जो घरसे निकले
ही नही

तो अलग अलग जगह एक्सप्लोर करो

www.ingramcontent.com/pod-product-compliance
Lightning Source LLC
Chambersburg PA
CBHW070528160726
48003CB00004B/1728